A Feminine Perspective

Margaret Pearce

A Feminine Perspective

First published 2024 by
GINNINDERRA PRESS
PO Box 3461 Port Adelaide 5015
www.ginninderrapress.com.au

Contents

Possession

I didn't believe them when they whispered I was behaving like a besotted idiot. It wasn't like a proper love affair with an ordinary mortal. He was never around for us to go anywhere as a couple. If I raved about how thrilled I was with the fact that I was the chosen one, everyone exchanged meaningful glances. No one had met him and none of my friends believed that I could possibly have a strong bond with such an invisible creature.

It had sneaked up on me so gradually, so subtly, that I wasn't aware of how much I was falling under his spell. For weeks, I pretended I didn't know about him or his relentless pursuit of me. His wooing was so shadowy and insubstantial that I wasn't really aware of him until I suddenly fell in the enchantment of love.

I was half asleep one night when I was thrilled to awareness of his presence. His touch was so gentle it was barely a whisper, but the thrill and excitement of that touch woke me with a gasp of pleasure. I sat up and switched on the light, but the bedroom was empty of his presence. There was only my husband snoring beside me. Yet he had visited me. I was too aware of his touch to be deceived.

Then there was the embarrassment of my body's bad reaction to him. I threw up when he first touched me and then I kept on throwing up. After a while, my body must have accepted him, and the nausea and horror of his touch vanished, and I at last stopped throwing up.

Whether it was the shadow of his influence or something more sinister, normal food started to repel me. For the first time in my life,, I craved bloody, half cooked steaks. Everything I craved had to be blood-red. I craved tomatoes, radishes, raspberries and even beetroot. I was losing weight for some mysterious reason. My good friends stopped being critical about how he was draining me and chased around for the only foods I could force down.

He didn't like the smell of cigarettes, so I gave up smoking. He took it as a personal affront that I needed to drink.

'There should be enough intoxication in my touch,' he mind-spoke to me.

I gave up drinking and even visiting anywhere I could be tempted to take just the one drink, or even one puff of a cigarette.

As the nights passed, his touch became less gentle and his presence more physical and demanding. I got to the stage where I stayed awake waiting for his arrival. It was a minor inconvenience that he was such a nocturnal creature and never around during the daytime hours for me to bond more strongly with him.

'You're starting to look dreadful,' my sister complained. 'And you're losing weight. Why don't you get some sleeping tablets and try to get some rest.'

I lied and agreed. There was no way I would sleep through his nocturnal visits. I didn't want to miss a precious second of the time he spent with me.

I did wonder whether he dreamed during his sleep periods, and if so who he dreamed of, but then I told myself not to be possessive. He was spending more and more of the nights awake with me. Towards morning, I usually dozed off, with my arm across his body, thrilled and ecstatic by how very solid and real he felt.

'I don't know about this love affair,' my mother grumbled. 'You shouldn't be so thin and listless. He's stealing all your energy and life.'

'He's welcome to whatever he wants or needs,' I admitted.

This got me a trip to the doctor, my mother glaring like a warden in the corner.

'Anaemia,' the doctor diagnosed.

I returned home with piles of tablets. They didn't work. I was still permanently exhausted. I was now spending most of the day in bed. Like my suitor, I spent the days sleeping and the nights awake with the ever present closeness and awareness of my beloved.

I was returned to the doctor in disgrace. He decided to inject the iron missing from my system. This seemed to work. I gradually felt more energetic and managed to stay awake during the day. I wasn't game to tell anyone, but the iron injections seemed to have made a difference to my beloved. After all, it was my blood and the extra iron injections keeping him so healthy and well nourished. He was so much stronger and more exuberant. His nocturnal games were getting rougher. Or maybe it was because I was now so frail I seemed to bruise so much easier. Fortunately, it was nowhere it showed, so I was safe from the further recriminations of my worried family.

Then the wretched iron injections somehow infected. I was in a lot of pain. I was bundled back to hospital. My beloved had gone very quiet for a change. I wondered if he was feeling guilty about his thoughtlessness in leaving me so bruised. He seemed to be sleeping the nights away as well as the days.

I closed my eyes, not wanting to see the worried face of the doctor and my mother's annoyed one. I was just so tired that somehow it wasn't worth the effort of fighting to stay alive.

Suddenly, my love affair was over. Why had I fallen in love so stupidly and with such an unpleasant, thoughtless and greedy lover? I must have been insane! I was going to die and for what? He just wasn't worth it.

'You have got to fight,' my mother's voice snapped unsympathetically. 'That parasitical freeloader has had his last freebie.' Her voice rose. 'Evict him, now.'

'It's nearly over,' the doctor whispered gently.

I shuddered. I knew I wasn't strong enough to evict my beloved. He had taken too strong possession of me. There was only death and oblivion in front of me.

'Possession is only nine points of the law,' my mother reminded me. 'Shove him out, now. We're here to help you.'

I blinked open my eyes. My relatives, the doctor and his nurse were around me in a solid comforting circle. It was painful, but I concentrated and at last ejected the parasite I had fallen in love with. The one who had possessed me so carelessly and thoughtlessly for the last ten months.

He was still fighting, thrashing around and bellowing with rage at being evicted from his comfortable existence. The doctor held him immobilised as he worked on him.

'No wonder you ended up so uncomfortable,' he said with a grin. 'A solid little devil and pretty strong at that.'

'Limb of Satan,' my mother warned. 'He'll bear some watching.'

I put out my arms and held him. He stopped bellowing. He seemed to have recovered from his indignation at being evicted. His scowl vanished. The blue eyes narrowed as he inspected me. He had such beautiful blue eyes. I felt myself drowning in them across the limitless void of eternity.

Unnoticed by the watchers, there was an instant acknowledgement and recognition between us. His face settled into beauty like that of an angel. Suddenly I wasn't tired, depressed or thinking about oblivion or death. I was instantly in love all over again.

'I love him,' I told everyone. 'He can stay.'

The Emergence of Spring

'I AM A NUT,' Patti wrote in her diary. 'NOBODY LOVES ME.'

The redheaded teacher was exasperated. 'I have explained that particular problem to you three times. Are you stupid as well as inattentive?'

The question required no answer, and the silence lengthened. She was gone! To a world where little girls were princesses, pampered and popular. The hectoring forceful tones broke through and dragged her back.

'Now try again, and for goodness sake, don't be so stupid.'

'I NEVER HAVE ANY FRIENDS. I SUPPOSE IT IS BECAUSE I AM SO SMALL.'

The writing in the diary was smudged where a tear had fallen.

'Hold your head up,' barked her father, in the tone he used with the laggards of the football field. 'Useless girls!'

Pattie remembered a time when the attention she attracted in her pretty blue dress and tiny black patent shoes pleased him. Now the expression in his eyes filled her with shame.

She knew she was plain, ugly and stupid every time his eyes rested on her. She always slunk past cringing, hoping he wouldn't notice, and grateful that the sympathetic shadows hid her from his attention. Sometimes, days went past before he noticed her existence.

'Twiggy,' mocked her dumpy little sister.

She hunched down, and tucked skinny legs further under her chair.

'I ACT LIKE A NUT SO PEOPLE WILL LAUGH AT ME AND LIKE ME.'

The writing was altering, rather like her figure. She could suck in her mouth so her two front teeth were prominent.

'Bugs Bunny,' giggled her little sister.

She rolled her eyes in appreciation.

The fist hammered down on the table, making the sugar jump. 'Stupid little twerp. Can't you concentrate on anything in that bird brain of yours? Where's the tea strainer?'

Patti's face closed in again, grew secretive and sullen, almost rabbity.

'ANOTHER BAD REPORT.'

The writing was ill-formed and despairing.

Her father slammed the report down, and glared at her. His irritation and hatred made his eyes bulge. 'You're stupid. You realise that, don't you?'

Patti nodded humble assent. Stupid, stupid, stupid. The refrain kept hammering. She must be stupid. So many years of being told so.

'You've always been stupid. Haven't you?'

She nodded. How could you argue against such compelling logic?

'Answer me, you little fool.' The veins stood out in a full-flushed tracery of purple on his cheeks.

'Yes, Dad.'

'Yes, Dad. Is that all you can say? All the money I've wasted on your schooling, and all you can say is, yes, Dad? You wouldn't get a job in a jam factory. You realise that, don't you?'

Patti's pale blue eyes were expressionless. If she pretended he was on television, and she turned down the sound, he would look comical, spluttering and gobbling with his face getting redder and redder.

Except there wouldn't be a television with colour exact enough to show the different nuances of skin tone that rose and fell across his face with the volume of sound.

'You give me a headache, you miserable little idiot. Try and do better next year, or I'll take you away from the school.'

The interview was over until next term. She bowed her head and waited for the parting threat.

'Another report like that and I'll thrash your miserable bottom to a jelly.' He jerked an aggressive jaw at her face. 'That's what my father did to me if I was ever stupid enough to have a report like that. I never had it easy like you.'

'I HAVE JUST FOUND MY VERY FIRST FRIEND. WE HAVE BEEN FRIENDS FOR OVER A WEEK.'

The writing sloped evenly in surprise.

Christine giggled. 'Does your dad do his block once a week, or once a day? Mine has regular eruptions just like a volcano. Mum and I time him.'

Patti's pale eyes deepened in amusement at the thought of someone having a dad who did his block and actually joked about it. It expanded the horizons of life.

'How much pocket money do you get?'

What a shameful thing to have to confess to a best friend. 'None. I walk to school and use my bus fares.'

'Does your mum know?'

'She gets a bit niggly because I am so late home every night. I tell her I'm kept in.'

Christine nodded agreement. 'I tell mine I'm on sweeping duty. They never check. Grown-ups are stupid.'

A fascinating concept. Were grown-ups stupid too? Her dad was always telling her mother she was stupid, incompetent, inefficient and neurotic, but she just thought fathers always said that to mothers.

Christine was generous. 'From now on, we share. I get plenty of money.'

The bliss of those months, hot pies and jam tarts all the winter, with uneaten lunches accumulating stealthily in the back drawer of her wardrobe.

'CHRISTINE STOLE FIFTY CENTS FROM MY LOCKER.'

The writing sloped and wobbled its hurt and dismay.

'I'll give it back.' Christine was remorseful. 'I needed it for my bus fare. Mum said I had to come straight home.'

'What did you do with the money for your bus fare?' Patti had to walk home in the rain.

'We had hot soup and doughnuts for lunch, remember.'

Patti was silenced. Christine's logic had a purity and justice all its own.

'No point either of us walking home in future. Always plenty of money around.'

'Where?'

Christine aimed a stone at a pert sparrow on the school fence. 'Around the lockers and blazer pockets.'

'That's stealing.'

'Little Miss Prude. What does it matter? Doesn't alter the taste of our lunch.'

'MY VERY BEST FRIEND ISN'T TALKING TO ME.'

There was heartbreak and misery curling the edges of the words.

'Lack of concentration,' went the school report.

'You don't deserve to go to a decent school,' raged her father.

A military-type commander, he sat in front of her, back erect. He tapped on the table with the report to emphasise his words. 'You have chances a lot of girls would give their eye teeth to have, and all you can do is loaf.'

Patti's tears trickled slowly down.

'Stop snivelling, and straighten your back.'

The tears came faster.

His obvious irritation and hatred was unnerving. 'Howling only makes you look more moronic than you really are.' His judgement was detached and remorseless.

Someone knocked. Her father put on his visitor's face, and she escaped.

'That your daughter?' asked the visitor.

Patti listened to the hearty laugh that was supposed to indicate good humour and amusement, but didn't.

'Going through the ugly duckling stage, I'm afraid.'

'I don't know,' was the surprising reply.

Blessed words. Patti stood behind the door pondering them.

'Give or take a few years, and she'll have charm.'

Charm? What was charm? She looked at her red eyes and pink nose in the mirror. Bugs Bunny! She sucked in her cheeks and the two front teeth sprang into prominence.

Her mother watched her and scowled. 'I've made an appointment to have your hair cut and set.'

Patti clutched at her hair. Her lank stringy hair was her; like her teeth and her eyes; a barrier through which she peered out at the hostile world. She couldn't face the world without the protection of shielding hair.

The hairdresser sniffed disgust. 'These knots have been in for weeks, perhaps months.'

'I don't want it cut,' Hysteria sharpened Patti's voice as she pulled away from the scissors.

'Nonsense, dear.' The hairdresser put on a professionally soothing voice, and yanked and tugged at the knots under the nape of her neck.

Patti was sullen and resigned under the dryer. The large rollers dragged at her sensitive scalp, but the hairdresser was firm.

'It's got to be in tightly to curl it, love.' The hairdresser had satisfaction oozing from her as she indicated the mirror. 'Now that's better than when you walked in.'

A scared look into the mirror. The lights glinted gilt across the curve of the neat pageboy, framing the bewildered face. It wasn't her at all. It was some other person. Someone she had no control over.

'Like it?'

She didn't give the satisfaction of an answer but fled from the shop with her head down, hoping against hope no one would see her. She reached the security of her home, with its overgrown garden, and shielding heavy veranda.

The dog's water bowl was cloudy with mud. Patti dunked her light floating hair in it, again and again until it was its lank dark self. She hid in the shrubbery until it was dry, and went inside.

'Wasting money on that little scruff,' her father sneered. 'Not much basic material to start with, is there?'

There was a date in the diary circled in red, and beneath it several exclamation marks.

'I DON'T WANT TO GO – I HATE DANCING.'

The writing had more shape, pale purple characters showing a touch of humour in the curves and squiggles.

'I won't dance,' she protested. 'I can't dance in these ghastly boots.'

A maxi dress hid bony knees and outlined the start of modest curves. The boots were long and white and eye-catching. Patti didn't want to be noticed.

'Wasting more money dressing up the ugly duckling,' sneered her father.

The next entry in the diary flowed gracefully.

'I WAS A BIG HIT AT THE SCHOOL DANCE. GOING OUT WITH A BOY.'

Patti stood straighter, and admired the clean blonde hair glinting in the mirror. At school, she had suddenly become a Personage. Someone who was actually going to the football with a boy. In the pecking order on the school perches, she was moving up.

Her father observed her popularity with approval. 'Takes after me,' he beamed. 'I've always been very popular.'

He took her to the races, and basked in the compliments paid her. He insisted she sit with him and smiled as he noticed the admiring glances. She still quaked when he yelled, but his noise was drowned in the silent homage of her courtiers.

'TODAY THE SCHOLARSHIP RESULTS CAME OUT, AND MY NAME IS AMONG THEM.'

The writing was blotched and childish with excitement and disbelief. She threw her shoulders back and breathed in the exhilarating air of success. It was a bracing climate to expand in. Her bitten nails grew into well-shaped ovals. She stood taller, full curves straining against the tight school dresses.

Her diary became disjointed and businesslike. Dates and places were listed against a bewildering assortment of boys' names. Columns of names, addresses and phone numbers marched down the pages.

'Of course,' said her father more loudly. 'I've always felt terribly protective towards Pattie. She was such a fragile little girl.'

However, no one took any notice. As was normal for the season of spring, the cocoon was splitting, and the emerging butterfly spreading cramped wings, to dry and harden in the hot sun of admiration and pleasure.

Kids All Fight

Billie looked at the fly-spotted mirror and pulled a face. The stain of the spilt orange drink was bright on the front of her school jumper and her skirt hem was down. There were no clean socks, and they were out of shoe polish.

'Move a bit faster.' Her mum sounded tired and bad-tempered. You could tell by the way the broom was being banged around the floor.

'I'll get a detention with dirty shoes.'

'You'll get a detention if you don't get to school on time.'

'Can I have some money to have my hair cut?'

'No.'

'Gee, Mum, now you're working, you ought to be able to afford me a haircut.'

'The quicker that dreadful cut grows out the better.' The voice rose into its bad-tempered pitch.

Billie slammed the door and escaped out of the gloomy watching darkness of the house. She knew the rest by heart, so why bother to listen?

'Hanging around with scum and riff-raff. No wonder your father won't have anything to do with you, or keep paying child support.' The sentences jerked out disconnected and blurred and faded into an accusing mumble.

Her mum carried on and on about her father leaving and her older sister Patti flitting off, but the money he used to send every month never got spent on decent clothes, so she was stranded in the ugly duckling mode forever. She resented the distaste always on his face when he saw her. Her hand strayed up to her bristly fringe and pulled at the lank hair around her neck. Nothing looked worse than a haircut growing out.

The seething rage rose and rose. She walked slower, contemplating her shabby shoes. If only her mother had let her have the high-heeled black boots. She could have worn them to school all the winter.

She had a good mind to skip school. No one would miss her. Her mates could volunteer she had one of her headaches. She would write the note.

Her mind traced the words. 'Dear Miss Henderson, Billie spent yesterday home in bed with a headache, yours faithfully.' It was so easy to forge the looped signature that petered out into the ineffectual wavy line.

She turned round. By now, her mother should be safely on the eight thirty train. If she went back, she would have the house to herself, all peace and blessed quiet.

Out of the corner of her eye she saw the blue car turn into the school gates. What if that old fool saw her? She quickened her pace, stumbling over the toothless spaniel belonging to the corner house.

Stupid animal! It should have been destroyed years ago. Why did elderly people hang on to their elderly dogs? She aimed a kick, feeling the satisfaction as her shoe connected. The breath went out of the dog with a satisfying whoosh and he limped off uttering high-pitched yelps. The blue car backed until it was level with her.

'Really, Billie, that was a spiteful thing to do.'

Blank round glasses, and foolish high-coloured face. Looked like a sheep. Great animal lovers, teachers were. Laying down the law like they were God almighty to helpless kids. It would be so nice to smash the smug stupid face to a pulp. To kick that flabby belly and stamp on the puffy feet stuffed into the new high-heeled, real leather shoes.

'He bit me, Miss Henderson.' She tried for a note of injury.

'Well, you'd better hurry. You'll be late for assembly.'

The car purred into the driveway. Billie followed, eyes downcast as she shuffled into line. Another day was beginning. She hated it, every miserable unpleasant minute and the interminable carping and nagging.

'Why didn't you do your homework?'

'I don't know, Miss Prenderghast.'

'Why isn't that assignment in?'

'I did it, and left it home, Mr. Jones.'

'Where's the rest of this maths homework?'

'I just couldn't understand what I had to do, Mrs Lucas.'

Idiots who said schooldays were the best days of your life were lying.

Billie's mind went resentfully to her cluttered evenings. It was all right for other kids. They didn't have their mother drinking with noisy pickups in the lounge, the kitchen so filthy there was nowhere to put a book down flat and a weird old aunt with an idiot son lurking in the background.

'When you stop dreaming, Billie, I want an explanation of how you reached this answer?'

'Isn't it right, Mrs Lucas?'

Awkward to be stuck beside Caroline, the class idiot. Half the time the stuff you copied was wrong anyway. Be better off making a stab at it yourself.

'The answer is right, but the steps you have taken to work it out don't give this result.'

'I must have calculated wrongly, Mrs Lucas.'

Stupid old fool. Wouldn't know what day it was. How did she get to be a teacher? Bet it was by sitting next to someone smarter than Caroline.

'Stay in after class, and I will check that problem over with you.'

'But my mother will worry if I don't go straight home.'

'Your mother gets home at four thirty, Billie. We'll finish before then.'

'Thank you, Mrs Lucas.'

Old cow! Who needs to know about working out maths? The gang will think I've slipped them up. Caroline will be wiggling around Gary, blinking her phoney eyelashes and he will forget I exist. Damn all adults! They should be wiped off the face of the earth.

'Don't tear that paper, Billie. You are a destructive child. Now pay attention.'

The clock ticked on and on. The voice went on and on, explaining, reproving, lecturing. Billie kept her head down and muttered agreement and comprehension in the expectant silences.

She escaped at last, but the schoolyard was deserted. She was breathing heavily by the time she reached the arcade where the gang met. It was empty!

The lump rose in her throat and she clenched her fists. Gary and Caroline together and she was out in the cold. They would be sniggering about her right now. Laughing because she never had any money to buy proper jeans or boots, or to keep her hair cut properly.

The shopkeeper gave her a suspicious stare as she sauntered through. She slid the chocolate into her bag even as she stared defiantly back. The warmth of her approval at her own cleverness boosted her spirits for as long as it took to eat the chocolate, but the black depression settled again.

Why did her mother have to take until four thirty to get home? This meant she had to hang around like an idiot all by herself. Not that her mother was anything to come home to, always whining and carrying on.

If she wanted money for a haircut, she would have to lift it from that shabby black purse on Thursday afternoon, before her mother did the shopping. God! It was awful to have a lousy mother.

Her feet turned her towards the railway station. If she walked very slowly, she might reach the station at the same time as her mother's train.

A train was pulling in. She jostled through the waiting crowd and kicked hard at the ankles of a girl blocking her view. The girl swore, turned and slapped her face hard.

Involuntary tears came to Billie's eyes, then suddenly, a startled joy. Her fists clenched. She had been struck and therefore could strike back. Strike back at something concrete and definite, not vague and shifting, like life, nagging, rejecting adults and shabby shoes.

The pleasure mounted as she thudded into the angry face with her bony knuckles.

And that's for the dirty socks I had to wear.

And that's because there was no boot polish.

And that's for being stuck next to the dumbest kid in the class and getting all my work wrong.

And that's for stupid Dad nicking off and Patti being old enough to nick off as well.

Her exaltation ignored the blows and kicks to her face and body. What did a few bruises matter? It was so good to hit at something. To hit back at all the dirty tricks life played on her all the time.

Suddenly, it was over. The girl broke and ran for her train, sobbing noisily as she scrambled into her carriage. Billie was left to stand alone, breathing heavily, feeling peaceful and drained.

Perhaps she wouldn't wait for her mother. She would go home. She might be able to get a few pages of her geography assignment done. She pushed her way out of the crowded station, ignoring the shocked comments.

'Vicious little bully.'

'Should be a police matter.'

Who took any notice of adults? They were a weird bunch of nuts. Kids all fight.

Metamorphosis

I opened the window and looked out. The night suited my mood. It was black outside. I was still and black inside. I felt it, like a deadness spreading through me.

The rain poured down, straight and steady like sighing beads. The drops showed silver as they fell past the light from the window, and the air was damp and perfumed; raw earth and gum trees that was what rain at night was all about.

A wind of discontent stirred the blackness inside me; stirred it like the occasional gust shook the trees outside.

Under the yellow of the light shade, the room seemed tawdry and shabby, scuffed-up mat, yuk pink, crumpled bed with the pillow still wet with my tears. The dressing table was the clutter of my mucked-up life. Four birthday cards toppled over; my cuddly doll with the stuffing gone from one arm sat across the three love letters from Geoff, spilt green nail polish and the last of the mascara.

'Why green nail polish?' she had wailed.

Was I thirteen only yesterday? It might as well be fifty. Thirteen is no age to be. My doll, tea set, and my fairy tale books belonged to yesterday. Yesterday was such a satisfactory secure age.

The mascara, green nail polish and the love letters belonged to tomorrow. I didn't belong in tomorrow. I was just pretending when I stepped across yesterday to tomorrow.

I was a fraud and a phoney and nobody guessed. Balancing across that fearsome gulf, I was scared yellow and nobody knew. I examined the reflection in the mirror.

'Mirror mirror on the wall, tell me who I am at all?'

Short hair and heavy determined features – boy or girl? Thirteen for a boy was a wide open adventure. Heavy strong shoulders and square capable hands that could hit a ball straighter and further than anyone else. No waist or hips, just the remorseless threat of brand-new curves. Girls had lousy lives. They weren't allowed to run free like a boy. I didn't want to be sheltered, protected and kept under lock and key like a caged dog, or should it be bitch?

The thought of locks brought back the family brawl in all its squalor. Presiding over the accusations and counter-accusations, She, uncomprehending, stupid and unjust, and It, shocked and equally uncomprehending.

'That horse you had to have is costing us a lot of money, and the least you can do is be grateful for what you've got, and more understanding about how hard it is to manage.'

'The horse didn't cost you, you pair of phonies.' Maybe I shouldn't have yelled at the top of my voice, but I was mad. 'You got a nice little nest egg from the sale of the old house. The jumping saddle is a bargain at five hundred dollars, and I bet you could find the money if you wanted to. I don't believe you can be such petty, tight-fisted, grasping parents.'

'You have no right to talk back to your parents like that.'

Why such outraged shock on the stupid faces?

Just one day after turning thirteen, to be punished like an eleven-year-old for telling the oldies a few of the facts of life. No right! No rights! I never had any rights. I wasn't eleven years old to be locked up without tea. I wasn't sixteen years old to leave home and go my own way.

The house was quiet. Wish I was old enough to have attentive boyfriends in expensive sports cars. Why do I only attract creeps with all their problems and who only ride pushbikes?

No television or wireless murmuring. She and It must have gone to bed. There was just the sighing of the rain as it gurgled and pattered on the leaves, and dripped past my window. The sound cooled and soothed the hot blackness churning inside me.

I stuffed the two pillows down my bed, put the cuddly doll where my head should be, and pulled the covers up. Artistic really, with the pillow twisted up to look like a hip. I checked the door was still tight shut and switched off the light.

The windowsill was slippery and clean. I dropped out on to the wet soft ground. The night was another universe, a strange new kingdom. The street lights were blurry halos and the road a shining black ribbon.

Everything was transformed. Neat pruned trees and stunted suburban hedges spread and extended into thorn thickets surrounding the humped shelters of savages; cowering from the blackness abroad.

Every step I took into the night changed me. I sensed the dark presence hovering over me, encouraging my metamorphosis into what! No longer was I poised in a no-man's-land between eleven and fifty, neither young nor old, or boy or girl. The blackness freed me. I was me, the original elemental me that didn't shrink and twist inside, trying to conform to daylight standards.

My hair plastered down over my eyes, clung to my neck and dripped the warm rain down my back. My runners squelched and softened to a sensitive extra skin. I felt the grittiness of the mud, and the roundness of the pebbles in the murmuring gutters.

Rain stripped the baby curves from my face, stinging across the hard line of cheekbones, narrowing and hardening my eyes. I altered and changed under its insistent moulding.

The wet knuckles of my hands gleamed large and white. I picked up the half-brick and threw, exultation at the extra energy flowing through me. The street light gave a distant apologetic pop, the sound smothered by the darkness that spread as it broke.

The lane was a black tunnel of space that I flew down like a bat. I hurdled the fence and ran down the paddock towards the formless blur of Bill.

He was warm and steaming out the smell of sun-warmed hay. A horse was a wonderful creation. Like a psychic suction pump, dragging out the choking lump in my throat, the bitter twisted stomachache and all the poisonous black unhappiness within me.

My breathing eased down. I was comforted; just the soft rain, the black night and the horse; sympathetic nostrils, acceptance and tolerance in each forward flick of his ears. He had warm placid flanks and his breath was the evocative smell of summer. Even his manure, warm and steaming, smelt of summer. I had a sudden urge to slosh my runners through just to spread the aroma around me.

The summer was over. I was thirteen. My summer was gone forever. Forever was a lifetime. I hugged him so hard that the beat of his heart drummed through me.

Bang, bang, boom, boom, it went; an insistent soothing drum. I buckled the bridle on. When I sprang on his back, the heat of his body and the rain welded my knees to his side. He was reluctant but under the stimulus of the beat pulsing through me, his walk broke to a trot, a canter, and then a flat out gallop for the fence.

The power of his jump surged through me as we hurtled over. It was like flying. As if we had plunged over a waterfall half-swimming, half-flying through insubstantial mist. Through my half-shut eyes, the street lights flashed past in a dizzying stream of rainbows and darkness.

The creek was swollen and noisy, hiccupping and muttering as it climbed higher up the bank. Bill jumped without lessening speed, and again his surge of power spread through me.

Was the horse part of me, or was I part of the horse? There was just the rain and me, and the warmth of Bill, flying along in a darkness edged with rainbows.

At the top of the hill, Bill, or was it I, stopped? The rain still poured down, the clouds low, heavy and edged with light, tumbling over and over with threatening rumbles.

Gazing up, I had a sudden shift of focus. I was riding a wild, bucking surging world, on the edge of the tossing abyss of eternity. Nothing else in the world, just Bill and I poised to fall upwards through the blackness.

A ragged edge of black cloud rolled off a sharp corner of moon. The light spread and the rain turned silver. The silver flooded over me. I shut my eyes and felt the silver go right through me washing the peace and belonging deeper in. The pressure of clouds squeezed the gap shut. There was the feel of warm rain on my face, warm horse under my legs and I blinked open my eyes to blackness.

It no longer mattered. I was me and I belonged. I wasn't sure where, but the confidence and trust were right through me. Bill knew. He turned and paced with steady steps down the hill, splashing through the creek back to his paddock.

He waited at the gate. In a kind of dream, I slid down and opened it. I slid his bridle off and put up the bar. He whickered a farewell and plodded off.

All the way home, up the long paddock, along the black lane, and across the black shiny ribbon of road, the soft rain washed the comfort and promise through me. By the time I climbed back through the window, the horsehair and stains were off my jeans, and the mud and manure off my runners.

The room was airless and stuffy, a confined prison smell, but it didn't worry me any more. I stuffed my wet clothes and runners as far under the bed as I could and got between the sheets.

In the morning, She would find them and start the usual puzzled complaints. It wasn't important any more. It didn't even irritate me to think about it.

Drowsing, I started to forget just what the promise was in the rain and black night, or what flash of revelation that the blinding silver of the moon revealed. I had metamorphosed, but I couldn't remember into what. All that was left was the comfort and security inside me.

The insecurity of fear, bitterness and unhappiness had been cleansed out of me. I was thirteen years old, and at peace with my environment. I cuddled my doll closer.

'Peace and happiness to my world,' I prayed, as the comforting blackness of sleep flowed over me.

Causing Malicious Damage

Fire is warm, cheerful and cosy. Even a nice blazing three-storey factory fire covering two blocks is blissfully cosy. It warmed me right through just watching.

How could I forget when it all started! It was over dinner that Mum told us she had got a job in the office of Goodhelp Makers Corporation. It was a big building that had overshadowed our district for years, but I had never actually noticed it before – what a joke!

It was the last decent dinner that Mum cooked, so I will remember it forever. We were all sitting around the table, Dad, Mum, my big brother, who had just joined the police force, and my next brother Gary, who spends all his time swimming and hopes to make the Olympics one day.

We had finished our roast beef, crisply browned potatoes and pumpkin, with baby carrots glazed with honey, and were spooning cream on to our lemon meringue pudding when Mum told us about her new job.

'They are a very caring company,' she said as she poured out our teas, remembering who took sugar and who didn't take milk. 'They have crèche facilities, hot midday meals, a very active social club and all sorts of support facilities for working mothers.'

The honeymoon lasted six months! Mum settled in raving about the beautifully cooked midday dinners for the staff. She became secretary, and then president of the social club, so the family spent a lot of weekends away, up at the company ski lodges, and then as the weather warmed, down at the special holiday camp for employees on the surf beach.

Mum put on weight and my brothers kidded her unmercifully. Over the years, what with all the rushing around she did, she was pretty slender for a mother of three kids. People were always taking her for my older sister – yuk!

She started watching what she ate – usually tomatoes or dry biscuits. The beautifully cooked meals she prepared when she flung in from work became rarer and then vanished completely. Especially if she had been attending one of the social club meetings and was running late.

'Anyone for a tomato sandwich?' she asked as she gulped her tomato and dry biscuits down before racing off to her next meeting or function.

It got so that it was hardly worth setting the table for a pot of tea and a plate of tomato sandwiches. It didn't worry me so much, or I suppose even Dad, but Joe and Gary took their food seriously.

I know perfectly well that it was weakness from lack of proper food that lowered Joke's immunity to that silly fat cow he moved in with. I mean, when you've got a couple of special extra spunky intelligent brothers, you want the best for them. It wasn't that I was jealous of her, but once he met her, our family relationship fizzled.

All Looney Louella could talk about were recipes. Ask her about anything else in the world except how to make pumpkin pie, chocolate éclairs, or Peking duck and she gave her silly titter. To make it worse, Joe, whose taste had been corrupted by all the Peking duck she fed him, actually thought she was wonderful! Talk about the way to a man's heart being through his stomach!

The way Mum wasn't cooking, there was no competition for the Peking duck, and Looney Louella for some reason hated me, so I saw my wonderful brother for ten minutes every four to six weeks.

He only dropped in to see us when his shift coincided with us all being home. 'And how's my favourite brat sister?' he asked, ruffling my hair without removing his arm from the vast expanse that passed for the waistline of Looney Louella. 'How's the power behind the social club?' he called at Mum. 'How's the head of the house?' to Dad, and 'How's the mighty swimmer going?' to Gary. He never listened to answers. Just walked through the house calling greetings, towing his fat cow along with him. Then he was gone again for another six to eight weeks.

No wonder I hated Goodhelp Makers' hot lunches. If Mum hadn't stopped cooking decent hot dinners, he would have still been at home.

Gary was the next to leave. I didn't begrudge him moving in with Christine's family. After all, he had known her for years and usually ate Sunday dinner round there. When Mum stopped cooking, he spent more and more time eating at Christine's. Soon he started staying the night at Christine's so they could both get an early start on their week-ends down the surf beach.

One day, he collected all his wetsuits and scuba diving gear and moved out forever. 'It's a lot more convenient to stay at the Smiths',' he explained.

'Of course, dear,' I heard Mum say. 'Silly for you to come home at all hours just to sleep.'

I couldn't believe it! She was actually pleased to get rid of him – my favourite hunk of twenty-year-old brother. She was relieved not to have to keep the refrigerator stocked and clean up the kitchen after his marathon efforts at cooking. I never realised she was so heartless and unfeeling!

I don't think she even noticed the absence of her sons. Goodhelp Makers had an active aerobic club going two nights a week and Mum was trying to drop her extra layer of flab. Also the social club was doing lots of fund raising for the local charities. Mum was too busy do-good-ing for the neglected children of the district to even notice her own ne-glected family.

The crunch came when Dad lost his job, muddled around cooking awful meals for a few weeks, and then ran away with the lady who cooked the Goodhelp canteen dinners.

I was so dumb! I should have realised when he stopped complaining about Mum never being home to cook and coming home later and later himself that something was going on.

The split-up of the family property came with horrific speed. Mum didn't fight anything! Said she much preferred living in a flat to a house.

I hated that flat! It was like an antiseptic shoebox, overlooking ugly red-brick walls, but Mum didn't care. She was never home anyway.

When I stayed with Dad, it was a disaster. He had moved into his lady's rambling Edwardian family home. She had a fat and stupid slob of a daughter not much older than me. And she had a toddler called Tabitha – yuk.

Tabitha was a spoiled brat who broke my cassette recorder and whined all the time. I couldn't concentrate on doing any study when I stayed there.

I couldn't even watch my own television shows, and that woman expected me to not only do my own washing and ironing, but also help clean up the permanently grotty house comprised of too many spooky high-ceilinged rooms connected with lots of dingy passageways. It was gothic! I don't understand how Dad stood it!

What made everything worse was that Dad was besotted with that grubby toddler. He was always bringing home toys and sweets and other surprises for her. I suppose I was lucky to get the calculator for my fourteenth birthday. It was the last present he ever got me!

Every night that little brat – and not even related to him – hurled herself at him like a tidal wave and stuck like glue; right through dinner, and afterwards until bath and bedtime. By which time, Dad was sprawled on the couch with his lady saying, 'Time for bed, Skeeter.' End of the evening! I was out in the cold again!

It was then I started to feel the cold. No matter how many jumpers I wore, or how much I turned up the heaters, I stayed cold. It was almost like frostbite. What froze me out more than anything about staying with Dad was seeing his lady parked against him on the couch. She was there in Mum's usual position. He even called her the same pet names as he used to call Mum.

The months went by and it got worse and worse. I got colder and colder. I couldn't concentrate on schoolwork any more. I didn't have my big brothers around to oversee my maths and Mum was never home to help me with my English. Dad never had time these days to discuss with me all the social issues we had to write about.

Nobody cared! Mum was busy with her work, the social club and other people's neglected children. The threat of her own redundancy meant more to her than her rejected redundant family. Dad had found a substitute cook and a new little girl to dote on. Joe moved in with Loopy Louella, who could cook like Mum, and Christine had at last got Garry into her clutches.

Goodhelp Makers Corporation had cold-bloodedly used their power and know-how to wreck my life for the greater glory of corporate profit. I was only one of the many tragic casualties of their agenda for undermining the sanctity of family life.

That nasty impersonal multinational institution emanated evil. Their poison seeped out around the district, tainting and freezing everyone into conforming little work units – pre-packaged ergs of maximum productivity.

Fire is a purifier! Don't they reckon that ashes are sterile? And I can't think of any building that needed purifying more badly than the Goodhelp Makers Corporation?

I felt like the sacred keeper of the flame when I trudged around with my little tin of kerosene. Amazing how economical it was to fire the whole building! Of course it helped that there were so many inflammable chemicals stored there.

I got into the building because I was meant to get in. Mum rushed off to aerobics and left the canteen keys in her spare purse. For a change, God was on my side.

I'm not a ratbag or any other sort of Jesus freak or crackpot. It felt so exhilarating and right to watch the flames dance, twist and roar their greed and abandonment into the black overhang of the clouds that night, but it doesn't make me an arsonist.

Burning that place down was my good deed for the night! Look at all the lives they have destroyed over the years. Look at all the people they put off before last Christmas, and people are more important than property, aren't they?

Fourteen is quite old enough to know about the importance of family life. I don't need any patronage from would-be do-gooders, or silly explanations from the shrinks. Until the past eighteen months, I belonged with an affectionate and close-knit family, Dad, Mum and my two big brothers.

The enemy has been humbled and I'm not sorry. Their destructive schemes for future family wrecking for higher productivity have been smothered in the ashes of their plant.

The heat generated by that fire has warmed me right through. It's the first time I've been warm since the whole miserable mess began, but I repeat again, I am no arsonist. I'm just a dedicated crusader against the wicked use multinationals had put their spare profits – hot mid-day lunches indeed!

The Liberation of Managing Director Barton

'That's the third personal assistant I've lost this year,' snarled senior managing director James Barton.

'You ought to pay them more,' advised his partner William Davidson. He was occupied in the important task of making the morning coffee for the staff of Barton and Davidson, Importers Ltd. 'Two sugars for the switch girl, no milk for the filing clerk. What about the new girl?'

'She doesn't drink coffee,' Mr Barton advised gloomily.

'Doesn't take coffee! Where are the teabags?'

'How would I know!' his partner snapped.

Mr Davidson handed his partner his coffee, put the other cups on a tray and carried them into the general office. He returned, shut the door and sipped at his coffee. 'Why do I always have to make the coffee?' he complained.

Mr Barton ignored the accusation hidden in the complaint. 'It's downright piracy! I advertise for a PA. I train someone until they're competent and what happens?'

'Someone is prepared to pay them what they're worth and you lose them,' Mr Davidson finished helpfully.

'Do you realise how my work is piling up?'

Mr Davidson gulped his coffee down and reached for his laptop. 'Try paying them a decent salary.'

Mr Barton slammed into his own office. His lip curled at the cascading mess of files on his desk and blinking red light on his voice mail. His sense of injury grew. His PA had been so well trained that he was able to indulge in a full day of golf and at least two leisurely lunch hours per week.

Now he was slaving away from eight a.m. to six p.m. with ten minutes for lunch and he was a managing director! He glared through the glass partition, envy in his heart. His partner's PA stared at the screen, tapping her way efficiently through her pile of work. She was Mr Davidson's PA with the over-award on her wages paid through Mr Davidson's personal account. He daren't unload his work on her.

He wanted someone intelligent enough to be his assistant, but not too ambitious. Someone who could be trained to share his workload. Someone who would give him a chance to lead the life of a senior partner and relax sometimes. It was hardly worth the effort of being the director the way he had to work at the moment.

He brooded his way through his messy pile of work when he had his bright idea. He rubbed his hands together with undignified glee and left the office with a buoyant step. He reached the old established firm of Wilson and Wilson Ltd, friends and competitors and the most efficient crowd in the city.

'Mr Wilson in?' he asked the receptionist.

'Yes, Mr Barton.'

Mr Barton was gratified. The girl remembered all the clients. Old Wilson was a good picker of staff. He would lure his PA away.

'You wanted to see me?' Mr Wilson looked peevish and suspicious.

'Just wanted to verify the figures on the carpet manifests,' answered Mr Barton in the breezy manner he always adopted when fronting up to old Wilson.

'We emailed them to you last week.'

'I didn't get them,' Mr Barton protested with a scowl. His PA had left without downloading the pile up of contracts and figures.

'I'll get Ms Dunne to go through them with you. I'm busy,' was the ungracious answer.

He vanished back into his office. Better and better, Mr Barton gloated to himself. If Ms Dunne is intelligent enough to assess the figures, she must be good.

A tall woman with heavy glasses and a pleasant smile came out. 'Mr Barton.' She had a low well-modulated voice. 'I'm sorry you didn't get the information I emailed to you last week. The accountant checked the profit margin of those figures, and I phoned the solicitor over clause eight.' She sounded apologetic. 'I know Mr Wilson was edgy over that clause.'

Mr Barton glowed with satisfaction; intelligent, quick-witted and hardworking. No wonder old Wilson had picked her.

'Actually, I was more worried about subclause two. Could we go into it more deeply over some lunch?'

Miss Dunne looked amused and nodded agreement. She collected a notebook and her handbag and strolled out of the office with Mr Barton.

Mr Barton put himself out to be lyrical about the friendly office and pleasant working conditions and prospects for advancement at Barton & Davidson Importers Ltd.

Ms Dunne was interested and then hooked. She promised to give a month's notice. 'After all, Mr Barton,' she explained. 'I do owe that to Mr Wilson. It is rather short notice, although Mr Wilson will understand I am entitled to better myself.'

Tactful too, noted Mr Barton with approval. She probably would be able to cope with those damn boring contracts all by herself. He returned to the office and explained his new acquisition.

Mr Davidson was amused. 'Are you sure you're happy about her joining the company?'

'Of course I'm happy. She's efficient and she's well up on law and accounting. She's what this place needs.'

'If you're happy, there are no problems then,' Mr Davidson agreed.

'I've offered her a third more than Wilson is paying and the same position in our firm.'

Mr Davidson nodded approval. 'Then she will be worth every penny, no matter how expensive she comes.'

Mr Barton settled to the month of handwriting contracts and the interminable phone calls almost cheerfully. In four short week,s all this would be over and he would be back to his golf, leisurely lunches and no writer's cramp.

The Monday Ms Dunne was due to start, Mr Barton took the first of what he hoped would be many late mornings. It was ten thirty before he reached the office. The desk outside his office was occupied by a faded blonde of indeterminate age with her head down typing furiously on the keyboard of a very expensive and late model laptop.

'Ah hum,' he cleared his throat. 'You're new, aren't you?'

She glanced up without her fingers stopping their flying speed. 'I'm temping – Miss Dunne got me in to help with the backlog.'

Mr Barton shrugged. He had anticipated that Miss Dunne would have been able to catch up on the backlog in her spare time. He reached the entrance to his office. The office furniture had been switched around and his two filing cabinets were gone! His desk and most of the floor was covered in files. Two young girls sat facing screens tapping in data from the files.

'You're separating my legal and mercantile contracts,' he roared.

One of the girls looked up. 'Orders from Ms Dunne. She said it was inefficient to have them jumbled together.'

Mr Barton breathed heavily and stepped over his jumble of office furniture and headed into his partner's office. Ms Dunne sat at the desk drinking coffee with Mr Davidson and smiled pleasantly. She stood up and left the room, shutting the door softly behind her.

'You're late,' his partner said. Mr Davidson sounded smug instead of irritated.

Mr Barton took a few deep breaths to settle himself down. No point in blowing his stack over trifles. 'You're getting on all right with Ms Dunne?' Mr Barton asked.

'A very efficient lady. She's already installed new software that is going to chop handling time on our contracts. Best thing you ever did was to grab her.' Mr Davidson sounded almost genial.

'You don't mind paying her the extra third?'

'It is a lot of money,' his partner admitted. 'But her law degree alone is going to save the company a lot of money.'

Mr Barton nodded complacently. If he hurried, he could probably catch old Bingley for a day of golf.

Mr Davidson spoke again.

Mr Barton at first didn't comprehend. 'What?'

Mr Davidson repeated a statement he obviously had been looking forward to making for some time. 'I said her extra third salary puts you out. It wasn't Mr Wilson's PA you pinched but his partner. She has bought into this company and as of this morning she is the new senior partner. Sloppy of you not to check her exact status before you offered her the position.'

Mr Barton still wasn't sure he was hearing correctly.

'Naturally I had to honour your commitment to her.' Mr Davidson watched the dawning horror on Mr Barton's face for a few seconds before dealing the body blow. 'She is of course, quite prepared to keep you on as her personal assistant.'

Mr Barton, ex managing director of Barton & Davidson Imports Ltd got up without a word and slammed out the door. The crash of the slammed door echoed in the air.

Mr Davidson finished his coffee and pondered on the odd twists of fate. Whoever would have thought he would have actually welcomed the progress of women's liberation right into his own office?

He reached for his laptop and the firm of Dunne & Davidson Importers Ltd settled to its morning routine.

The Heat of the Noonday Sun

At midday, the sun casts no shadow, so why should I have even suspected?

The shadows puddled beneath everyone, as if hiding from the fierceness of the sun. Behind the shelter of my sunglasses and hat brim, everything was two-dimensional, stripped and faded of colour, black and glaring white.

The street was crowded. We had bumped against each other. He apologised. We exchanged casual words about the crowd and the unseasonable heat. Inside the building, my companion still appeared two-dimensional, black hair and black eyes in a white face.

He entered the lift with me. I pressed the basement button. My brother ran the boilers of the big department store and I was lunching with him, as I often did. Once down, my way led behind the crowded shopping area, past the busy cafeteria, across a deserted passage and as far as a narrow door. My companion followed close behind me.

'Are you lost?' I asked, spinning around to face him. 'This area is not open to the general public.'

I didn't really assume he was following me. I was so drab and colourless that I merged into any background unnoticed.

'I don't happen to be the general public.' The thin line of his red lips relaxed into a smile. His teeth were chalk-white and regular and a dimple shadowed one side of his mouth.

'You work around here?'

'Down the back.' He gestured along the passage. 'I organise the trendy models for the store windows.'

I turned into the small door leading to my destination and he kept walking along the passage.

'Yeah,' my brother said thoughtfully as he poured me a cup of tea. 'Heard some of the window dressers bitching about how inconvenient it is to keep the stuff this far down. New security measure. The window models are going missing.'

'Who would want to pinch yucky old window models?'

'Twenty dummies went missing this week. The store detectives are on the prowl.'

'Bit hard to walk out of a store with a window dummy under one arm,' I said. 'Think I met one of the new window dressers. A dream in black and white, including hat.'

'Acker Wolven. The other window dressers don't like him, but he is extra special. Check his front window on the way out.'

The big feature window was a summer beach scene. The window had a reality of atmosphere that slowed the passing crowd to linger and stare with understanding smiles. There was a painted backdrop of surf, with a cartoon figure painted waving frantically in the waves. In the foreground, a curvaceous blonde and a taller more slender brunette displayed bikinis. The three lifesavers gathered around them, backs to the painted waves, displaying jutting muscles and bleached toothbrush haircuts to the two girls. The petite blonde model had sloping shoulders and the curving out hips of a real person. Even the taller, brunette dummy had a realistic-looking shape and her feet looked flat and ordinary in the strapped sandals.

My opinion of the new window dresser rose. It was very clever to use such average-looking models. I studied the latest fashion in bikinis thoughtfully. They were vivid and eye-catching. Not that I even wanted to wear anything as daring or attention-getting, but they presented a sort of this-could-be-you challenge to Ms Average female viewer.

The following week, the two store detectives stopped me on my way to my lunchtime visit.

'This place is out of bounds, Brinda,' the older one said. 'What are you doing here?'

Kerrigan looked a typical stereotyped detective. He was craggy, red-faced, overweight and overage. Under his shabby jacket, his favourite Fair Isle knitted waistcoat stretched tightly over his beer gut.

'I'm visiting my brother, the boiler attendant, to have lunch with him. Still losing stuff?' I asked.

'Four more dummies gone this week.'

'Want to search my bag,' I offered, opening up my handbag with its two jam lamingtons, purse and make-up.

'Just keep your eyes open,' Kerrigan said and he and Bill Stevens strolled off.

Once settled with my cup of tea, the conversation turned to the new window dresser.

'You would think all these dummies going missing would inhibit him,' I said. 'His window displays use crowds of models.'

'And he doesn't use them more than once,' my brother said. 'Management is very happy with his talent.'

That night, I had to rush back into the store to buy some replacement pantyhose. I thought I saw Kerrigan walking out the door. I remembered his timetable from when I had worked at the store. This time of night, he was supposed to be on duty. I called him. He ignored me and kept on going. He wore an odd peaked cap pulled low over his head. For a second, I doubted if it was actually Kerrigan. He hadn't even turned his head at my call and the build and the walk were all wrong.

He turned in the street. The jacket swung back showing the faded hand-knitted Fair Isle waistcoat. I called again, but he was gone.

'Heard that Kerrigan's missing?' my brother asked the following day. 'He and Bill Stevens were heading down to the sports department and Kerrigan just disappeared.'

'I saw him leave the store last night just on six,' I said.

'You positive?'

Was I? The hurrying figure had seemed taller and slimmer than Kerrigan, but I had recognised the jacket and distinctive Fair Isle waistcoat. I repeated what I had seen to Bill Stevens, who was very stressed and the police, who seemed equally stressed.

'I mean, he was following me down the back stairs,' Bill kept insisting. 'His footsteps behind me suddenly sort of stopped. I looked around and he just wasn't there!'

'Could he have ducked off into one of the toilets or storage rooms on the landing?' I asked.

'Why would he do that? We were going down the flight of stairs to the sports department and he just wasn't there any more,' Bill insisted.

The days slid past. Kerrigan stayed missing. The unseasonable heat dragged on. Everyone was working back at my office. As the supervisor, I had to organise the taxis to ferry late workers home. The spate of missing persons being listed by the city papers was making everyone jumpy. Except me, of course. I had nothing to get jumpy about. I was so drab and colourless that I never attracted any attention, welcome or unwelcome.

'You could make a lot more of yourself if you had the guts to move out of those cover up nothing sort of clothes and show off your decent figure,' my brother had once criticised, irritated at my lack of friends of either sex.

'This is my choice,' I had said. 'I'm not into tarting myself up to attract losers.'

My brother had shrugged and dropped the subject. He was aware of my lifetime shyness and embarrassment at any sort of attention.

I bumped into Acker Wolven again a few days later in the passage that led to his workrooms.

'I've been admiring your racing carnival window display,' I commented. 'Your window displays certainly have originality.'

His window had captured perfectly the atmosphere of a racing carnival. I had almost drooled over the group of smartly dressed models. They had made me feel unsettled and for the first time in my life resentful of their self-assurance and perfection.

What would it really feel like to be the centre of attention? To be so perfectly groomed; to wear high fashion clothes with such complete assurance; to accept the homage and admiration of the well-dressed men and the envious respect of all others as a divine right?

The window dresser had not missed a single detail. There was even the final touch of a jolly, heavy-set, smiling detective holding the shoulder of a small urchin with a scared expression on his face, his hand still in the open purse of one of the elegant racegoers.

'I look for originality,' Acker said. 'Without originality, a window display is banal and trite and who looks even twice at a cliché?'

'Very clever indeed,' I praised.

The window dresser repelled me, but his talent and brains were to be respected. The dark holes of his eyes looked down at me and the red gash of mouth softened into a smile.

I was suddenly transfixed; staring at the way that mouth moulded in such perfect curves and the dimple which appeared at the side of the nothing of his face. For a second, I fantasised about that mouth. My brother had hinted that the window dresser was gay! That made that mouth a terrible waste in that pallid uninteresting face.

'Body language,' I said, trying to distance myself from my undisciplined imagination. 'You adjust your models to show body language. What a clever person you are.'

'And what a perceptive person you are,' he praised in return.

We had reached the narrow door where we had parted the last time. I opened it. The black holes of his eyes suddenly had a greedy light behind them as he studied me. They were almost pretty eyes, heavily fringed in jet-black lashes, with fine drawn brows above them.

'A very perceptive person,' he repeated. 'With lots of hidden depths as well. How unusual!'

I stepped back into the open doorway, obscurely glad my brother was within earshot at the top of the iron ladder. There was something gloating and suddenly unattractive about the too pretty face of Acker with that too red carnal mouth.

He stepped after me and lowered his mouth on mine. I stood as if hypnotised. I didn't want that mouth on mine, but at the same time I yearned for it to connect with me as if I had been dreaming of it all my life. His mouth was cold, so cold that all feeling and sensation fled.

He turned and strolled along the passage. I followed as if on an invisible lead. I stepped down the three steps and through the door into the small room cluttered with window dummies and racks of clothing, and paints and backdrops. He snibbed the door casually behind me.

I was frozen beyond shivering. I stood unresisting as he put down my ordinary leather handbag, slid off my sunglasses and hat, unbuttoned my shapeless brown linen dress and slipped off my sensible flat brown shoes.

He reached for one of the dummies along the wall, buttoned it into my dress, adjusted my hat and sunglasses on the featureless head and slipped my shoes on to the feet.

He snapped his fingers. Something wrenched inside me. Suddenly I was staring across the untidy room at the rigid stance of a mousy short-haired woman with unnaturally blood-red pouting lips, wearing sensible cotton bra and briefs. The loss and anguish started as I realised she was wearing my face, only it was as blank of expression as a mindless idiot.

The window dresser unsnibbed the door, put the handbag on an arm and gave a casual wave. I walked with jerky steps, except it wasn't me! I was trapped inside the dummy! It walked me through the door, up the three steps and along the passage. I felt each effort as the rough cast dummy's arms and legs were pushed into movement. I struggled to slow the legs, but they carried me onwards.

'Brinda,' my brother called from the top of his ladder as I went past the narrow still open door. 'Changed your mind about coming in for lunch?'

I was screaming inside, but the rough-cast throat had no vocal cords. The stiff limbs moved me on. I walked through into the main part of the store, up the lift and out the main door to the crowded uncaring street. I boarded the fourth tram.

I stared out the window. I could still think and feel and I was scared. The detective Kerrigan was so macho that it was a joke? What if Kerrigan wasn't really so macho? What if the window dresser had been waiting in one of the small rooms off the back stairs? Had Kerrigan been snared by that too red mouth as I had been? What had happened to him? What was happening to me?

The tram threaded its way through the meaner industrial suburbs. People got on and off the tram. No one even looked at me. I was used to being invisible, but now I was only a faceless dummy. Surely someone should notice how odd I looked?

The tram stopped at a crossroads. My stiff body stood, and stepped down from the tram, walking jerkily along the lane to the back of a dingy warehouse. I slid open the rusting metal door and stepped inside.

The two men packing the long narrow boxes turned towards me. They looked like clones of Acker Wolven. More than one of him, how odd, my frozen captive mind thought.

'Another consignment to pack and sent out,' one said.

The legs marched me stiffly and remorselessly towards them.

'Also Known As the Wolf has led us to good hunting grounds,' the other said as he unbuttoned my dress and threw it and my hat into a bin full of crumpled clothes. Among them I spotted a familiar shabby jacket and faded Fair Isle jumper.

Also Known As, Aka, makes Acker, my shrieking mind thought.

The clone took out the credit cards from my purse and threw the bag into an open incinerator. 'Selling the dummies is a lucrative side-line.'

Sideline! What were these creatures if the money made was just a sideline?

The dark head lowered to slip off my shoes and throw them in the bin.

'It's centuries since we have fed so well,' the other one agreed. He snapped his fingers.

Something wrenched inside me again. I was snapped back into my own body in the cluttered workroom of the department store. The window dresser was sorting through a rack of costumes. I tried to move, to breathe and to scream. I was still frozen!

I stared at the clothes he was selecting. The iciness of terror gave way to a dreamy approval. The window dresser did have perfect taste and I had to acknowledge it. Of course they were not the sort of clothes I would ever have worn, being myself, but somehow Acker had liberated me from myself and I was an exciting stranger, a perceptive quick-witted mysterious female.

'My next window display is men's evening clothes,' Acker said.

He dressed my body with impersonal tender loving care in a dress of clinging red lace, pulling the neckline lower to expose more of my breasts and making sure that most of my upper thigh was exposed through the deep slit of the skirt.

My modest underwear was gone and I didn't care! He knelt at my feet to slide on the high-heeled strappy sandals. My rigid body softened and swayed towards him. I had never had a man kneel at my feet before.

'I see you as a lady of the night, all red lace and passion, but sharp-witted as well.' He fitted the jet-black wig across my head. 'You're going to love and enjoy every second of my new display.'

I knew I was. There was only smug satisfaction and pleased anticipation tunnelling through the frozen remoteness of my being. I felt exactly like Cinderella! There was a destiny ahead of me! I was going to bask in the focus of an entire city's awed admiration. I was going to be lusted after and desired and it was going to warm me right through.

For the first time in my life, I was going to be daring, beautiful, admired and the centre of attention. All that red lace was going to be so flattering! I had been a frozen captive all my miserable, unhappy existence. Acker Wolven and his species, whatever they might be, were doing all of us unhappy misfits a great favour by recognising our imprisoned inner selves and liberating them!

There was no horror, apprehension or fear in my realisation that it had been Kerrigan in the racing carnival window, or that after their stint as window dummies, the missing people were ending up being consumed, or something even worse, by weird and artistic predators.

Not yet!

Some of My Best Friends Have Been…

I'm a secure and sensitive new age sort of male. I enjoy going out on the town on the usual male ritual bondings, but I like women as well. Some of my best friends have been women.

My first experience of women was my mother, saddled with us three kids by her various suitors. She was a pretty female with an incredible talent for lavishing affection on all and sundry. I have always had a soft spot for females with that sort of talent.

Miss Hopkins was the second female in my life. She was forthright in her speech and actions, and you always knew where you stood with her. 'Irresponsible young piece,' she had snorted about our pretty young mother when she snooped out that we were neglected and abandoned. She bullied the neighbours into keeping an eye on us until we were old enough to be independent.

My sister vanished with some Romeo pretty early in the piece and my brother ran away. He was very resentful about being cooped up by some do-gooder.

I had to admit that I wasn't game to run away, not from Miss Hopkins. She had personally nursed me back to health. When I was better, she found me a home with Mrs Jenkins and her three boys. I fitted in all right. Mrs Jenkins was pretty good at coping with teenagers.

I was the first to leave home. I set up in business as a pest exterminator. I did all right.

My first live-in relationship was just one of those accidents. She was older than me, attractive and intelligent. I was rushing across her path on my way to shelter one wet night when I bumped into her.

'Yuk! How wet can you get!' she had exclaimed. She looked at me more closely. 'Like to come in and dry off?'

I accepted the invitation. Then I went down with a nasty chest infection after getting so wet and couldn't work. She fed me, paid for my medicines and nursed me back to health. Our relationship deepened into something sincere and genuine.

She had lots of friends. Most accepted me as her new house partner and were sociable and friendly. Only one of her friends took a dislike to me. When he realised I shared her bed, he lectured and lectured her about me.

She seemed to take a delight in upsetting him. Once in his presence, she kissed me full on the mouth. He launched into a full-scale row before being told to go.

'He's upset because he imagines he is emotionally involved with me,' my lady explained. 'You should never get emotionally involved with people. They stuff up your lives as well as their own.'

He took her out for dinner behind my back to apologise. She arrived home with a smug smile and a ring on her finger. I was stunned to realise he had been my rival all along! She had been using me to make him jealous!

'This doesn't mean you have to go,' she had coaxed. 'He promised to accept you in my life as well. He can love us both. I'm sure threesomes are more emotionally healthy than twosomes.' She paused, looking embarrassed. 'He refuses to share my bed with you but I guess you should be comfortable enough on the couch.'

I stared at her in horror. The couch! After all we had been to each other! Of course when he moved in, I moved out. I've got my pride after all. I wasn't kinky enough to share a female. I didn't hold it against her of course. She was one of the nicest and most intelligent women I had ever known, and we remained good friends.

For a while, I was working next door to a single mum with young kids. The warmth of her love and caring for her kids exuded through her house. I used to watch her all the time, but she wasn't into casual relationships.

Anyway, I got my opportunity to get acquainted. I heard her

screaming one day and rushed over. One of those large hairy outdoor spiders had her bailed up on her front porch.

'They aren't really pests,' I explained as I dropped it outside. 'They do a lot of good keeping down piles of insects.'

She didn't listen of course. She confessed to a phobia about spiders and was grateful enough to invite me in for a drink. Our acquaintance ripened. We had a very stable relationship. I would have stayed forever if it hadn't been for that silly fight.

She had a part-time job. I worked the odd job here and there, but there was never really enough to eat, and the three kids came first. I was hungry and one day ate the steak she had left out to defrost.

'It was to have fed the five of us, not just greedy stupid self-centred you,' she had wailed.

I shrugged and stalked out in dignified silence. Who wants to hang around someone who can be so nasty? I didn't need to be told how stupid, thoughtless and greedy I had been to knock off the only food in the house.

She admitted later she had been tired and bad-tempered, and forgave me for being so thoughtless. She was the most dedicated, selfless woman I had ever come across, and my life has been enriched by knowing her, and our friendship has lasted untainted.

The next female I moved in with was what all my friends predicted I deserved. She was into channelling, astral travel and other new age hobbies, and good-looking in a sort of weird way. She made the running when she spotted me.

'You are the most handsome, arrogant, macho male I have ever seen,' she gushed. She was very into being blunt and forthright about what she wanted. 'Come live with me and be my love.'

I had a ball! She cooked for me; she cleaned for me; she sang me to sleep and she sang me awake; she cut my nails and cleaned my teeth. She sulked if I went out to work, and sulked if I went out with the boys for a night. She didn't want me to improve my mind, or my manners, or my speech. She accepted me totally as I was, which of course was perfect.

She didn't expect me to be nice to her friends. In fact, she gave up having friends. I had never had anyone focus total dedication on me before. We were totally indivisible, like a single unit. We slept together, we ate together and we read together. We listened to music and watched television together.

'When we die,' she said hugging me tightly, 'our love will transcend death.'

That stirred me from my smug acceptance of her obsessive devotion. Did I want to die with her and transcend death? Did that constitute true love and friendship?

I puffed my way down the steps from her first-floor apartment to the garden below. The cane chair by the fishpond creaked under my weight. I stared at the smug round face and podgy form reflected in the water. My only exercise had been waddling towards the tempting beautiful meals prepared and offered with such love and affection.

It was terrific to be the focus of someone's whole life, but was it healthy? I was likely to have a heart attack carrying all this extra weight, or come to a sticky end if she decided to cement our love with a suicide pact. Was it healthy to have someone do everything for you?

I fled! I became increasingly fit with the distance I put between us. I had learned something from her. She had loved me so passionately and obsessively it had given another dimension to my life and I respected her for it, but I worried about the idea of death pacts and perfect oneness. I didn't feel satisfied that our relationship had explored the dimensions of true friendship.

After that, being wary of one-to-one relationships, I stuck to one-night stands with the sort of females who understood the rules. It was a lot safer than getting emotionally involved.

It was during this stage I drifted into a communal house. I originally went in for a few days, but ending up staying for years. I had never struck a place with so many pests. They had the idea it was wrong to kill anything, so the mice, the rats, even the possums had a ball. I got rid of every mouse, rat and possum, and even the cockroaches.

They weren't into using money for payment but they kept me housed and fed. It was a friendly, easy-going casual sort of place, with people coming and going all the time. There were ageing war veterans, runaway teenagers, womanisers, misogynists, potters and artists, buskers and bikers and the odd disenchanted cult follower.

There was plenty of companionship all the time. The guys were great heroes who got boozed and bragged of their deeds in the commercial world, on the road, at war or in beds. When they got too boring, I moved to spending time with the women of the place. They all seemed to have a down-to-earth common sense and humour that was a lot easier to take.

One hair-raising night, one woman didn't make it to the hospital on time. It was the first time I had I witnessed a home birth. The ambulance arrived in time to congratulate her friends who had delivered the baby. I was never impressed by the bragging of the guys after that. To me, women putting their lives on the line and going through all that trauma for the sake of a future generation were the real heroes.

Came the day when a cheeky rat walked right past me. I had been feeling off colour for a while, and realised I had been doing more dozing around the kitchen than working. I forced myself on my feet and went searching.

A family of rats had installed themselves under the old incinerator. My health had deteriorated and badly! I wasn't strong enough to dig them out! The other guys ignored the rats, and the women were into letting everything live. I felt shamed and useless.

It was time to move on. The guys of the house agreed. It was the women who got upset and pleaded for me to stay. Their loyalty and sincerity was very touching, but I had my pride. I sneaked off one night when no one was around.

I was too sick to work, ineligible for dole or sickness benefits and life got worse. I became a derelict tramp drifting from shelter to shelter.

One day Miss Hopkins snooped past. 'Tom,' she exclaimed as she recognised me. She always called me Tom, although it wasn't my real name. 'You look dreadful! What have you been up to?'

She scooped me up, took me home and nursed me back to health. She was as bossy and forthright as ever and still the terror of the neighbourhood. There was a bit of talk about me staying with her.

Everyone knew Miss Hopkins had strong views about ne'er-do-wells like me, but she seemed so pleased with my company that I stayed. She had retired from teaching and seemed to me to be a bit lonely, although she never admitted it.

I put in my time all right. I potter around the garden in the mornings and every evening I go visiting. I have made lots of friends over my lifetime, most of them women. I am always made very welcome and it is nice to keep in touch with everyone.

Miss Hopkins doesn't like me wandering off during the evenings, but I make a big fuss of how pleased I am to be back every night, or early next morning and she settles down again.

'You're a comforting creature to have around the house, Tom,' Miss Hopkins admits. 'I'm so glad you've decided to stay, although I never was that fond of cats before.'

I nodded agreement. As I say, some of my best friends have been women.

A Matter of Willpower

The indicator swung round the dial and then steadied. I was down another three kilos.

'No cakes, takeaways or sweets,' my doctor said. 'Just a matter of willpower and you'll feel a new woman.'

I did feel like a new woman. No more shapeless shifts for me. The tailored fitted clothes suited my new image as a well dressed woman of decision and willpower.

I passed a cake shop. The window was full of fattening rubbish, vanilla creams, fruit buns, coffee scrolls and éclairs. My only reaction was amused tolerance. I paused to examine the display.

The plate of chocolate éclairs was right at the front of the window. They were enormous! The chocolate icing had a rich gleam, as though it was so fresh it hadn't had time to set properly.

I swallowed, as though the dry biscuits I had for lunch were still stuck in my throat. Inside me, a pain started, as though the cottage cheese and olives I had eaten with them still gave me indigestion.

I stepped back to get the reassuring reflection of my trim figure. By some accident of light, the plate of chocolate éclairs sprang into prominence, nakedly exposed on the front shelf and leering at me.

Shutting my eyes, I willed thoughts of crisp lettuce and freshly cut tomato into my mind. The insidious memory of vanilla-flavoured cream mixed with rich dark chocolate invaded my taste buds.

I opened my eyes to admire my reflection, but the entire window seemed dominated by the plate of chocolate éclairs.

Every detail etched itself into my mind. The way the piped dark chocolate rippled so thickly across the top. The vanilla cream had been squashed in one corner and had oozed out. A few fresh crumbs of the sponge finger had fallen to the side of the plate. The dusting of icing sugar on the base of the éclairs made me breathe hard.

A moan was wrenched from me. A passer-by paused. My respectable appearance must have reassured her, for she walked on.

I was hardly aware of the door banging behind me as I entered the shop.

My voice seemed to come from a long way off, forced out from the depths of my deprivation and lust.

'One dozen chocolate éclairs, please, and I'll have some of those cream buns with the raspberry jam.'

All decisions in life were only a matter being in control and, of course, of willpower.

Nightmare

It wasn't really the fault of the children that their mother ended up in that place. It was just one of those things.

The night it happened it had been wet and stormy. Jasmine, Gerry and Matthew watched *Nightmare on Elm Street* until its violent and gory end. Their mother knitted and their dad read his magazine.

'Bedtime,' their dad said, without looking up from his magazine.

Matthew was first in bed. The book on his pillow had a cover was of two scared children running from a fiery-eyed skull.

'*The Curse of the Cemetery Owl*, by B.R. Tine,' his mother read. 'Sounds nasty.'

'He's a terrific writer, Mum,' Matthew said. 'You ought to read it.'

'All right,' his mother promised.

Directly over Jasmine's bed was a shrunken head. Her mother winced.

'Fab, isn't it!' Jasmine said. 'It's a genuine copy of a shrunken head.'

'Dear me,' said her mother.

Gerry's was putting together a plastic skeleton. The skull had an evil look about the eyeholes, enhanced by black crayon.

'Swapped my old cricket bat for it,' Gerry said proudly.

'Dear me,' said his mother and returned to the lounge room.

She read *The Curse of the Cemetery Owl* with a fascinated horror.

An urgent knocking sounded at the door.

'Gotta go out and give George a hand,' her husband reported. 'He's bogged his car in the lane and needs it towed out.' He left.

There was a deafening roll of thunder. The lounge room lights and the television flickered out. The mother groped her way to the emergency supply of candles. She lit one and took it with her into the bathroom. She set the candle on the hand basin. She looked into the mirror and gasped. Gaunt haggard cheekbones and deep hollows where eyes should be stared out at her. She lifted the candle higher. It was only her reflection! She blew out the candle and got into bed.

The storm went on. Then she heard someone or something rapping at the window.

Fear rose. Perhaps someone with vacant eyes, drowned waterlogged flabby skin and dark hair slicked lankly against a gory splintered skull was trying to get in. Perhaps it was a lank bloodsucking shadow, revived to unnatural unlife by the abnormal electrical storm? Perhaps it was a homicidal maniac with an axe, escaped from prison and stirred into a bloodthirsty frenzy by the storm?

She sat up and lit the candle. She stalked across the room and flung up the blind in one swift courageous gesture. The candlelight illuminated a hollow-eyed creature standing on the other side of the glass. A misty dark shadow that faded at the bottom into nothingness. A groping claw-like hand banged against the window.

She let out a frightened screech and dropped the candle. She slammed down the blind and flung herself back into bed under the heavy doona.

She couldn't stop shivering. The wind – or she hoped it was the wind – howled and moaned around the house. The rapping on the window became more agitated. The cold across the pit of her stomach spread.

The rapping at the window stopped. The wind stopped. It became deathly quiet. The rapping started up again at the front door! Then it started at the back door.

Was something without a proper throat or tongue hoarsely calling her name, seeking her out? The rapping, the knocking and the rattling of the doorknobs had stopped. Had whatever foul thing the storm had raised gone?

In the silence, the click of the faulty latch on the bathroom window sounded as loud as a pistol shot. The window swung back with its distinctive squeal. The scrabble of something pushing its way through the window was shockingly loud.

She broke free of her paralysis of terror, crawled out of bed and groped for the candle and lit it. She raised the candle. She had no control over her limbs. Despite her terrified protests, they had a life of their own.

She walked like a sleepwalker towards the bathroom and whatever foulness that had been seeking her. In the bathroom, something in the deeper shadows by the window something moved.

She raised her candle, without hope and dulled by fear. Something with slicked-down hair, blood dripping down the side of the mangled face, drowned waterlogged flabby skin, sparks darting from the hollowed shadows where eyes should be stepped forward into the light of the candle.

She screamed and collapsed in a dead faint. There was the sound of running footsteps along the hall. The television and the lounge room lights went on. The deeper shadow flicked the switch. The bathroom light went on.

It blazed on the bewildered face of Gerry and the annoyed wet and bloody face of his father.

'I thought your mother was asleep when she didn't answer my knocking,' his dad explained. 'I climbed in the bathroom window to avoid disturbing her.'

'I heard you knocking, but thought Mum was still awake,' Gerry apologised.

'I slipped and cut myself on the car, the torch packed up and I went face down into that boggy patch on the side of the lane.'

'Better climb under the shower before Mum sees you,' Gerry said. 'You'll scare the daylights out of her. Did she slip on the floor or something?'

'Or something,' his dad said, looking worried as he kneeled to pick her up.

She was aware of the soaking wet, chillingly cold arms around her and the putrid smell. With a shudder of horror, she knew that whatever had been out in the blackness seeking her had claimed her!

She made a last determined effort. She screwed shut her eyes even tighter, and pushed herself deep deep down into black oblivion of unconsciousness, to cower behind an impenetrable protective shield against the loathsome thing embracing her.

And stayed there.

The Siren Call of Autumn

'Annie.' George sounded brisk and far away. 'James will be home for dinner and my plane won't be in until ten. Make my apologies, will you.'

'How long is he down for?'

'Going back in the morning. Make up the spare bed. It's the only chance I have to discuss those new securities you're interested in.'

'Goodbye,' Annie said.

Long-distance calls were such a waste. She went down the passage to make up the spare bed. It was nice that George and James were such friends. They had grown up in the same community. He had married that timid little mouse Brenda.

Annie flung the pastel sheet across the bed remembering with contempt Brenda's first fiasco of a dinner party all those years ago. She and George often wondered what old James had seen in her. Brenda had died of some ailment or other. Her mind wandered on to what to give James for dinner. He liked his roast lamb and green peas. Perhaps an apple pie and cream for sweets? They didn't see much of old James now he had started his new business interstate.

Down the street, she paused at the second-hand bookstall. She wanted something for James to read for the evening to make him feel more at home. A paperback caught her eye with its lurid cover. A half-naked brunette with flowing hair and dark frightened eyes crouched behind a square-jawed man with a gun.

Once upon a time. Jimmy Watson had been a gangling twenty-year-old mad on detective stories. She had been barely eighteen. He had red hair and freckles and he stammered. He worked and went to night school and barely had the money to buy her a milkshake. Yet earnest young Jimmy Watson somehow was extra special.

Deep inside her, something stirred and woke to nag with a warning twinge. She placed a hand under her bulging diaphragm where the emptiness pulsed, spreading apprehension and a vague yearning. Her double chin trembled with the intensity of her need.

She wanted her nice hot pot of tea, an aspirin and some chocolate cake. She suddenly needed nourishment. She wasn't one of those women trying to retain their figures with haggard, sagging faces. She searched the plump reflection in the shop window with approval. The cold emptiness inside her receded.

In the afternoon, she consulted her wardrobe with a frown. The blue slack suit was her favourite, but the loose top made her look grand-motherly. If she wore her black, she would have to wear corsets. She decided on the slack suit. After all, blue was her most flattering colour and the slack suit was discreetly expensive.

She had dished up and put the plates in the food warmer by the time James arrived.

'James,' she greeted with a smile as she opened the door to his knock.

He flushed a dark red into his grey beard and clasping her hands, kissed her heartily. 'How do you do, Annie. My word, you never change, do you?'

'Neither do you,' she laughed as she looked up at him.

He had filled out of course and there was something aggressive in his still erect posture, but the eyes under the sandy brows were still those of twenty-year-old Jimmy Watson whose ambition was to be a great detective.

'Dinner's all ready. Now put your things in the bedroom and come and sit down.'

She was just picking up the oven cloth when she had a sudden at-tack of vertigo. She straightened and leaned against the cupboards, breathing shallowly. She felt quite odd, detached and light-headed. What was wrong with her?

James didn't seem to notice her apprehensive silence. He complimented her on her cooking, and ate with obvious enjoyment as though the evening was the same as many others he had spent there.

The shadows stretched and danced around the candles, and the light sparkled off the silver. Annie and George were great believers in living in a civilised manner with decent table settings and good furniture. It made for comfort and relaxation, but somehow, lying in wait like a prowling animal, the tension grew, feeding on the well-cooked dinner, the silver and the steady flame of the candles.

'Pour yourself a whisky and get me a brandy,' Annie ordered as she stacked dishes into the dishwasher.

A brandy would settle her stomach. She didn't feel herself. The meal hadn't dispelled the aching emptiness and apprehension in the pit of her stomach.

'Come and sit down, Annie.' James ordered. 'You look a bit pale.'

Annie settled herself on the lounge and reached for her brandy. A little tremor ran through her as their hands touched. Suddenly a ghost was in her gross elderly body trying to get out! She felt the tapering fingers through the broad red hand holding her glass. She crossed her legs in discomfort. She wasn't a fanciful woman, but through the fat thighs and the heavy mottled legs that rubbed against her blue slacks were the long smooth legs narrowing down into neat ankles and high- arched feet.

'Your feet have got breeding,' a twenty-year-old Jimmy had whispered as he kissed each arch.

'Someone will see you. Don't be an idiot.'

'Pardon?' James queried.

Annie shook herself. Had she really said that or did she just think it?

'Sorry, James,' she apologised. 'Did you see the paperback I bought for you?'

James put his head back and laughed and his bald head caught the gleam of the candlelight. 'Blood and thunder and glamorous women. I still enjoy reading them, you know. When no one's looking of course.'

He tilted his glass and stared at the candle flame through it. 'You know, Annie, to me you represented all those glamorous and exciting girl-friends those dashing, quick-witted, courageous detectives ended up with.'

Annie tossed her head with pleasure and flung back her hair. Not the carefully tinted, short waved hair, but the long dark brown locks that had once tumbled down her back in such luxuriant abandon.

'Very good for my self-esteem,' she teased. Even to herself, her voice sounded different, lilting as though it had a signature tune running through it.

'You talk like a Welsh princess,' Jimmy had once whispered against her cheek, such a smooth silken cheek.

James was still looking through his drink. 'Remember the way I used to sign my letters when I was going through the Saint craze?'

'The stick figure and the halo.' Annie remembered.

The vertigo and the detached light-headed feeling flooded back. Love letters, always starting, 'Beloved, come fly with me,' to the beach picnic, or walks in the country, or wherever. Of course she never took penniless Jimmy Watson seriously even when she was eighteen and by the time he was established with a promising career, he had married that simpering Brenda.

She shrugged irritably. Inside her large body, she felt the small high-pointed breasts lift with the movement. She stood up and started pacing, up and down the deep carpet. She paced from the mahogany cocktail cabinet and back to the glassed in bookshelves with the gold printed leather volumes.

The emptiness spread through her body and up into her heart, causing a deepening anguish. Perhaps she was going to have a heart attack? She sensed Jimmy watching her as she walked. Not her large comfortable bottom, discreetly hidden under her loose top, but her swaying hips sloping out below her narrow waist.

She paused to put her glass down, staring at the ornate gold-framed mirror. Somewhere in the shadows, lost in the plump complacent face, large dark eyes too big for the wilful narrow face stared back. She felt confused and off balance. The pounding wrenching pain had reached her throat.

'Come and sit down,' James ordered. 'I thought you had outgrown that.'

She sat down beside him, and spoke with an effort. 'Sorry, James. I feel a bit edgy at the moment.'

'You always were a restless bint,' he said as he patted her hand. 'Don't know what old George thought of you when he married you.'

Detached and out of control, she felt the well-shaped hand hidden in the thick ageing skin return his clasp. The pursed lips relaxed in the full sensual shape she used to outline with purple lipstick and then Jimmy Watson was kissing her, freckles flushing as they always did.

'How can you have changed so little over forty years?' he muttered.

'How can I?' she asked in anguish and the years crumpled like ramparts of sand before a raging tide of hunger.

By the time George had opened the front door at ten o'clock, humming to himself; his bewildered eyes traced an adulterous trail of discarded clothes to his very own bedroom, where the prim unused flannelette nightie flung its sleeves in mute appeal from the carpeted floor.

The Efficacy of Prayer

It was between pension week and the gas and electricity accounts were overdue.

'Drat!' said old Granny Sullivan, surveying her empty cupboard. She had paid her rates out of the previous pension, but if she paid her gas and electricity account, her bankbook would be as empty as her larder.

Of course her two and a half chooks, two leghorns and the one bantam were still laying, but eggs tasted better with a nice slice of fresh bread and butter. Everything also tasted better cooked, and without gas and electricity, she wasn't going to be able to cook.

Her daughter raising her five kids alone never had any money. Her suggestion about how much money could be saved by moving into her spare room translated as an unending stint of babysitting.

She could borrow off her son. Only he kept suggesting that she sell up and move into a place that catered for senior citizens.

'Live with all those elderly people,' she had scoffed. 'Besides, I like my house.'

'This district's pretty rough,' her son pointed out. His nice car had lost an aerial, three hubcaps and its nice logo the last time he visited. He was very judgemental about her district.

'Lived here all my life and nothing bad ever happened to me,' she had pointed out.

'Because you've got nothing worth pinching.'

She pretended not to hear. 'I know everyone around here. I've seen all the kids in this district grow up.'

'Into crims and jailbait,' her son snarled.

Granny Sullivan sighed. She could have light, heat and cooking facilities, or she could have food to cook and nothing to cook it on. She would withdraw the money and go by church and pray for guidance.

She took off her apron, put on her shabby black coat and hat, put up her umbrella and headed out. She emptied out her bank account. Once in church, the usual peace and serenity worked its magic. She hadn't made a decision either way, but she felt comforted. She knew that God was looking out for her.

It was still raining when she came out. She headed for the small shopping centre, still undecided about paying bills or buying food. As she passed the small pub, a body hurtled past her and splashed into the high running gutter.

'Sorry, Mrs Sullivan,' the bouncer called. 'Didn't notice you walking past.'

'If you were throwing him at me, you missed by a mile,' Granny Sullivan retorted. 'All that booze spoiling your aim?'

The bouncer, a large young man Granny Sullivan remembered from when he was a cheeky kid, grinned and went back inside.

'Shame on you, Bill Cummings,' Granny Sullivan scolded. 'How can you be drunk before midday on a Monday morning?'

'Turned up for work and we've all been sacked, haven't we,' the drunken Bill snarled as he scrambled out of the gutter. 'What's the missus gonna say?'

'She hasn't lost her job as well, has she?' Granny Smith was tart.

Bill was always drunk, always losing jobs, or starting strikes. Half the time he and his mates were either picketing their workplaces or their ex-workplaces and still not getting paid. If his wife ever got sick of supporting him and their swarm of kids, he would really be in a mess.

He scrambled to his feet cursing monotonously. He cursed the weather, the bouncer, the pub, his missus, the place he had been sacked from, and his bad luck in life.

'You shouldn't take the Lord's name in vain, Bill Cummings,' Granny Sullivan scolded. 'One day, you'll have to stand up in front of the Lord and account for all that blasphemy with your immortal soul.'

The reply set off another string of foul swear words interposed with the suggestion that Granny Sullivan was a meddling old fool who should mind her own business.

'Religion is the opiate of the masses,' Bill raved on. 'There's no such thing as an immortal soul. When you're dead, that's it. Finito!'

Granny Sullivan felt herself ruffling. How could that man not believe in God? Suddenly, as if God was standing right beside her, the solution to Bill's problems was plainly in front of her. 'Are you saying that you don't believe in an immortal soul, Bill Cummings?'

'Garbage,' Bill scoffed.

'Will you sell me your immortal soul that you don't believe in?'

'Definitely senile,' Bill jeered.

Granny Sullivan clutched at her bag. There was exactly two hundred and fifty dollars in there. One hundred dollars and ten dollars for the gas bill and one hundred and forty dollars for the electricity bill.

'I will give you two hundred and fifty dollars in cash for your soul that you don't believe in,' she said.

'You got that sort of cash?' He put out his hand.

'Not so fast,' Granny Sullivan said briskly. It was fortunate she had office training from the days of her youth. 'You have to sign a contract that you have sold your immortal soul to me.'

'And you'll give me two hundred and fifty dollars in cash?' Bill asked.

Granny Sullivan fossicked in her bag and withdrew her small notepad. She ripped off the front page with her small shopping list. 'Kneel down so I can use your back to write out the contract.'

Bill knelt down. It was awkward, holding her umbrella up and writing with her biro on the pad she steadied on his back, but she managed.

'Here,' she said as he stood up. 'Received from Melinda Sullivan the sum of two hundred and fifty dollars in cash for Bill Cummings's immortal soul. dated this thirty-first day of October. Now you sign it.'

'Give me the pen then.'

'It's got to be signed in your blood,' Granny Sullivan said. She produced a darning needle from her bag. 'Prick your finger and sign it.'

The man's ruddy face paled.

'Two hundred and fifty notes,' Granny Sullivan reminded.

Bill pricked his finger and managed enough blood for a messy signature.

'Very good.' Granny Sullivan put the note into her bag and produced the money.

'You belong in a loony asylum,' Bill gloated as he counted the notes and swaggered back into the pub.

Granny Sullivan kept on her way home. She didn't have the money to pay her electricity or buy any food, but she had an instinct she had done the right thing.

A white van pulled up.

The driver popped his head out. 'Hi, Mrs Sullivan. I was doing some deliveries and was given some leftover bread and margarine. I was bringing them to you. Want a lift home?'

'Very thoughtful, James.'

James had joined one of those odd sects. At least, the sect believed in immortal souls. As he drove, he spoke fluently about the real meaning of the Bible and God's design and the necessity to protect your immortal soul from sin.

Granny Sullivan then told him about purchasing Bill Cummings's soul, and how Bill was a drunken blaspheming non-believer.

'Gosh, Mrs Sullivan. Our sect is into saving souls. Would you sell me his soul so I can take it to the elders for praying over?'

'I don't know if that would be ethical, James,' Granny Sullivan worried.

However, James was so keen to acquire the purchase rights of Bill Cummings's soul he offered her four hundred dollars for the receipt.

'I mean, we are the right people to have it, and the elders will pray over it most sacredly and reverently to bring him to the light,' he insisted.

He drove off triumphantly, the document in his top shirt pocket. Granny Sullivan, now four hundred dollars richer in cash, had a comfortable dinner of eggs and bread and butter.

Later that evening when she had settled to her favourite telly programs, there was a thunderous knock on the door. She opened it, peering through her security door at Bill Cummings and his wife.

'Can I have it back? Here's your money?' Bill gabbled. 'Enie made up the rest I hadn't spent.' He seemed sober but looked wild-eyed and stressed

'But you don't believe in immortal souls.' Granny Sullivan was puzzled.

Enie clenched bony fists and glared at Granny Sullivan through the security door. 'Everyone knows you're too hard-headed to waste money so you must have got something of value from my Bill,' she accused.

'Something neither of you believe in,' Granny Sullivan insisted, more and more puzzled.

'I want it back whatever,' Bill whined.

'I resold it to that James who joined that weird sect,' Granny Sullivan confessed.

'I want it back,' Bill whined again.

'So go talk to James,' Granny Sullivan suggested as she shut the door.

'God certainly does work in mysterious ways,' Granny Sullivan mused to herself. 'Enough money to pay my bills and enough for food to last until my next pension. How can anyone ever not believe in the efficacy of prayer and immortal souls?'

And whether Bill Cummings ever got back his immortal soul that he didn't believe in is another story.

Takeover

George Smith's hoped for takeover of the newly widowed Penny Pastel was not getting anywhere. 'Why isn't she interested?' he complained to his friend Horry. 'I'm a widower, she's a widow. We should marry, merge our assets and live happily ever after.'

'Try more sentiment and soft-soaping,' Horry suggested.

'I'm not into that soppy stuff.'

'Hire someone who is.'

George cheered up. 'Good business practice. Management should always delegate.'

Horry suggested Amadeus. Amadeus was newly come to the district and seemed short of cash. He was retired and did odd jobs around. He was tall and slim with blue eyes that twinkled.

It was rumoured that Amadeus wrote poetry. George approached him. Amadeus suggested flowers every week with suitable softening-up couplets, at the shocking price of ten dollars per couplet. George flinched, but agreed to pay.

George scowled at the 'come live with me and be my love and we will all the pleasures prove', but wrote his name under it.

He thought 'My love is like a red red rose that's newly sprung in June' even worse, but signed it anyway.

He didn't bother to read them all after that one, what with having a delicate stomach. He just paid over the ten dollars and signed them as requested.

'Something in all this poetry garbage,' he confided to Horry. 'Penny danced three times with me at this week's social and was real nice.'

One Friday bingo night, George was on the receiving end of lots of sympathy and understanding from Penny Pastel.

'This is it!' George exulted to Horry. 'Sentiment and soft soap do work after all.'

Saturday afternoon, George was shocked to receive his invitation to the marriage of Penny Pastel and Amadeus Wilson.

'Why?' he demanded.

'I am fond of you, George,' Penny Pastel confessed. 'And I loved your kindness in sending me flowers every week with a lovely poem, but you are a one-woman man.'

'And you're it,' said the desperate George.

'No,' Penny Pastel said, shaking her head. 'It wouldn't be right to marry a man who still grieves so deeply for his first wife.'

'She was a lovely lady, but she's been dead two years. It's you I care for,' George bellowed.

'It's her you will always care for,' Penny Pastel corrected. 'I respect and admire you for your constancy to her. Besides, Amadeus has been so supportive and comforting.'

'With my flowers and poetry,' George snarled later over a consolatory beer with Horry. 'That sneaking Amadeus guaranteed the roses and soppy love poems would work, every single line of them.'

'The poems and the roses did work pretty good,' Horry agreed. 'She's marrying Amadeus, isn't she?'

'Suddenly, she went cold on me,' George mourned. 'That treacherous Adey has made a successful takeover bid on the nicest widow in town.'

'What was the last poem before she cooled off?' Horry asked after a thoughtful silence. 'Maybe you insulted her or something in one of them.'

George checked the last couplet sent. He opened his mouth to read. His face reddened. He spluttered, choked and spluttered again. Horry took the page to read it aloud.

> MY HEART BURNS WITH ETERNAL FIRE
> LOVE WITH JOY I WILL ALWAYS DESIRE.

'Ah!' Horry said. 'Bit of a trap, all this delegating. Amadeus wasn't to know that your first wife's name was Joy?'

Transition

There was infinity of space between the bed and the window, the polished floor reflecting a shiny sky. Sometimes, the sky was grey and sometimes white. It was the only changing thing in the ward.

'Have you taken your tablets?'

The insistent voice caused Tabitha to blink vague eyes.

It was hard to remember how long she had been in this still room. Days slipped into weeks, accelerating into a blur of confused time. Her nieces and her grandnieces had visited, but she kept forgetting their names. Which was silly, as her two nieces were named after her own sisters, except the niece named Elizabeth was nothing like her sensible stolid young sister Elizabeth. Tabitha pressed her lips together tightly at the remembrance of the embarrassment of her stupid niece Elizabeth. Janine was the sensible one of course.

Her other niece Annie had not bothered to visit since she heard that the house had been willed to Janine. Tabitha gave a grim smile, and the wistful something in the greyer shadows sniggered in agreement at the memory of what Tabitha had left to her niece Annie.

How long did it take to die? How long before the screens were raised and she was hurried out behind closed doors? Odd that death was such an embarrassed obscene visitor in this nice hygienic hospital. An ever-present attendant, mentioned with oblique references, hinted away in a flutter of trivialities.

'Kidneys going,' grunted the young doctor.

He had the chin of a fighter. The battles he had lost in that hospital since she had been there! He fought so hard, armed with his drugs and oxygen tents, but his adversary mocked him over the battlefield of aged bodies and failing organs.

Tabitha tried to get comfortable. Her body ached so with all the needles and tubes. If only that young man would fight his everlasting battles on his own arena, the vital healthy bodies of the young, where he had some chance of winning.

'I want a special on tonight and I could need the oxygen.'

There was a stir in the ward as he marshalled his ranks. Ridiculous young man with his clenched jaw and bad-tempered frown. He should be out playing cricket in the long summer evenings, not dancing attendance on old ladies preoccupied with dying.

Tabitha's rheumy eyes stared down time. So much of her had died in her lifetime. What was left was hardly worth bothering about.

A lot of her had died when her Ted marched away. Even after all these years, she still felt a pang when she remembered those square shoulders and the back of his arrogant head. She had only been eighteen and they all said she was young enough to get over it.

'It happened at Gallipoli,' she announced to the grey square of window, and her voice quavered. The pain in her heart twisted again with the suffocating loss.

'Another attack.' The young man was back again, chivvying up his forces in the bright room.

Tabitha drew in painful shuddering breaths. All those gallant young men had marched away. So few had limped home from their great adventure to marry their sweethearts. Her Ted was gone and she joined the great army of spinsters mourning the loss of their productive futures, gone with their loved ones.

Her spinster friends devoted themselves to nieces and nephews and ageing parents. At least she had the excuse of her ailing young brother Harry to fill the empty spaces of her life. Young Harry, too young for the Great War and then too ailing, had occupied her life from the death of her Ted.

Only now, young Harry was gone. He had wheezed and gasped his way through that long cold winter, to fade away in the spring. It was then that the insolent weeds encroached and triumphantly conquered young Harry's cherished domain, until there was nothing of Harry left in the wilderness beyond the kitchen door.

When she fractured her hip and had that dreadful flu that left her gasping like a stranded fish even when she was supposed to be recovered, the doctor had looked thoughtful and kept visiting.

'You'll be more comfortable in the home,' the social worker had said firmly, after her hip had nearly healed.

She left the run-down family home, surprised by the intensity of her desolation. Life had lost its savour. She packed her best flannel nighties and her favourite family portraits. Young Harry in his first breeches and cloth hat, all big eyes and solemn face; her mother Sarah; her stern, bearded father Jeremiah; the little miniature of her oldest sister, who had died young and was said to have been the only beautiful woman in a family notorious for plain daughters.

Where had they gone, vanished like wood smoke on a windy night? No one remembered them except her. She sighed and twisted her head away from the grief of being so alone.

'Sedative.'

What was her life when she had spent such a long time dying? She opened her eyes in shock. Surely she was just eighteen, her waist tiny under her corsets, giggling behind her hand with her friends.

The drugs faded her aching hip like a bad dream. She was floating, barely remembering the indignities of catheters and bed pans. She looked around the room. The young doctor was still there and two nurses. She shut her eyes, willing them away.

She had a sudden nostalgia for her Ted, hazel eyes creased in amusement, or even young Harry, stammering his excitement when he got his apprenticeship as a gardener. She wanted the comfort of familiar faces around her. Ted had promised to return and he was a man of his word. Everyone knew how steady and reliable he was.

'Ted,' she whispered.

The young doctor scowled, and his jaw stuck out even further. 'Wandering. It won't be long.'

Tabitha opened her eyes again. Outside, the window was darkness. How comfortable she suddenly felt, relaxed and tranquil. Of course Ted would return! He was a man of his word! She should never have fretted and grieved all those long years.

She felt a fading trace of pity for the white-coated man leaning over her. She was on the side of the victor now and this battle they were winning. She was leaving this filthy muck behind, floating off free as an autumn leaf on the enticing wind of death.

Acknowledgements

'The Emergence of Spring': a version was published in the anthology *On the Offbeat* Volume 2, Carbon Productions, Victoria, September 1987.

'Kids All Fight': a version was awarded third prize in A.E.A. Pat Veitch Competition 1974. A version was held for use in *Engwenda Magazine* 1977.

'Metamorphoses': a version (as 'Fifteen is No Age to Be') was commended in Australian Artists Queensland short story competition, July 1984. A version (as 'Metamorphosis') won first prize in the Bendigo FAW short story competition, November 1998.

'Causing Malicious Damage': a version was commended in *Positive Words* short story competition. A version was published in *Her World*, Singapore, March 1980. A version was broadcast on *Words & Music*.

'A Matter of Willpower': a version was published in *Waterline News*, August 2017. A version was used in *THEMA* magazine, June 2022.

'Nightmare': a version was published in *Swag of Words*, 2006.

'The Siren Call of Autumn': a version was published in the anthology *Stories of Her Life*, Victoria, 1979.

'The Efficacy of Prayer': a version was published in *Sparx*, SWWVic, issue 5, December 2020. A version was published in *FreeXpresSion*, New Year 2022.

'Takeover': a version was published in *The Waterline News*, August 2016. A version was published at https.facebook.com/Tales-stories-books and writing, July 2021.

'Transition': a version was broadcast on Radio 5UV, SA, 19 August 1977. A version was published in *Calling All Housewives*, Victoria, May 1978.